Guilty at the Rapture

Guilty at the Rapture

Keith Taylor

Hanging Loose Press
Brooklyn, New York

Published by Hanging Loose Press, 231 Wyckoff Street, Brooklyn, NY 11217-2208. All rights reserved. No part of this book may be reproduced without the publisher's written permission, except for brief quotations in reviews.

Hanging Loose Press thanks the Literature Program of New York State Council on the arts for a grant in support of the publication of this book.

www.hangingloosepress.com

Printed in the United States of America
10 9 8 7 6 5 4 3 2 1

Cover art by Ann Mikolowski
Cover design by Ben Piekut

Library of Congress Cataloging-in-Publication Data available on request.

ISBN: 1-931236-61-5 (paperback)
ISBN: 1-931236-64-X (cloth)

 Produced at The Print Center, Inc. 225 Varick St., New York, NY 10014, a non-profit facility for literary and arts-related publications. (212) 206-8465

Table of Contents

This book is for my sister, Sherrill Pearson

GUILTY AT THE RAPTURE

All things good would rise
into air, pulled from dirt and sky,
from cars left driverless
below, slamming into trees.

That would be my first clue.
On my ride home from the river—
burning on my gold Schwinn
and sucking hard on a mint to smother
the newspaper cigarette I'd just smoked
in a stand of scrub willow—
I would have to dodge
machines abandoned by vanished Christians,
glorified while driving back from work
after centuries of trial.

I would know a final loneliness
before I screamed through the back door
and found supper smoldering over gas.
My parents gone. Even my sister—
only a hair less guilty—
called to her celestial chorus.
I would be alone in a world
of smokers, crooks, murderers,
of moviegoers, gamblers and sex fiends,
left, at last, alone in a world
without one hope of grace.

GRANDMOTHER TRIPTYCH

1.
The Holy Dance

We hear they've opened
an old folks' home
in her name. We're proud.

We remember her black dresses
shining like Bibles, her hand
moving lightly over our backs and arms,

her prayers, long and touching
(I timed her once—
sixteen minutes of grace before supper).

Only an old man
who moved south, to Nebraska,
remembers how she moved

and the hard burning
behind her
at the barn dance

where she turned,
fast,
spinning,

her white dress swirling out,
quicker, until everything
pulled in, even light.

2.
Her Creation Story

Because he died young,
because he never saw his child,
because he was the only man she had,
she nurtured her scrapbooks,
her photographs—

> *He smiles,*
> *pulling his broad-brimmed hat*
> *low over one eye, playfully*
> *riding the plow. Behind him,*
> *miles of prairie grass.*

She forgot the hours
when he climbed down
to vomit into the fresh furrows.
She forgot the body stretched
out on three bales of hay,
the mortician who cut open
his head with a hacksaw
and found a clot
the size of a child's ball
at the base of his brain.

She remembered his death
only as a fog lifting
slowly at sunrise,
leaving her in new light
alone with a child.
She guarded his letters—

> *I'm doing my own seeding,*
> *have about 90 acres in,*
> *and the first sowing*

(wheat) is up nicely.
I'm hard after the balance.
I have a good fat outfit
this year.

She wrote poems
"For Father in Heaven"
filled with the sea
she'd never seen.
Her farmer turned
Christian voyager,
his mouth set firm
against the taunt of death.

His eyes grew greener,
his hair thicker,

until she finished her picture,
her phantom,
the father for her child.

3.
Taking Down Her Hair

My sister
draws out the pins, mother-of-pearl combs
that catch everything together in
their polished

tines. The old
woman's hair cascades down, its public
Mennonite composure suddenly
shimmering

light, falling
in liquid strands almost to the floor.
My sister gets to stroke the brush through
that hair, holding her breath while she swims
gently past

the snags. I
can only curl up on the big red
bed and watch the silver hair trickle
through my sister's fingers, tumble past
grandmother's

back. Sister,
let me touch it. Let me hold my hands
in that cold
gray water.

POPPAWOOD

My sister and I slid across the floor in our stocking feet. It's what kids are supposed to do, despite grandmothers worrying about slivers or broken china. Our living room was long and narrow, the front end of a converted barracks. Mountain View Bible College, where my father taught Pauline Epistles and Homiletics, bought the building from the Canadian military in 1947, after the Germans were defeated and there was no longer a need to send prairie wheat farmers off to Dieppe, the Pas de Calais, Juno Beach. The Bible College couldn't pay my father much, but we lived for free where lonely young men, hardly more than boys, had laughed or lain terrified before shipping out. My sister and I would run as fast as we dared then slide to the couch at the far end, crying "Poppawood, Poppawood, Poppawood . . ." as many times as we could while still sliding. Sometimes our father would pretend to be the monster who would devour us if we ever stopped saying "Poppawood." We didn't talk about the soldiers who had lived in the barracks. We never heard, not once, the lamentations of their ghosts.

ALTAR CALL

One sin: enough to free the leather strap
kept in the top dresser drawer curled
around my father's socks. One little indiscretion
across the trailer park, between the grain elevators,
way past the tracks, will always come home.
No one smiles at supper. My sister's eyes
speak sermons on the coming retribution.

But there's one way out. If Sunday comes
soon, I can beat that sin, its whipping.
I can walk down the hushed aisle
Just as I am without one plea
humming around me.

My friends, who should be praying,
squint through their lashes, nudge each other,
say, *There he goes, getting saved again.*

At the altar, before God, before everyone
I know in the wide world, I confess
quietly, and the deacons kneeling
around me overhear my slide from grace:

My Heavenly Father:
I stole Dad's tithe to go to the movies;
I smoked a whole pack of cigarettes in the granary;
last week I called Rocky Listle a son of a bitch.

Redeemed from fire, saved from that good
whipping, I feel for one long hour
what might be the faint certainty of faith.
My elders can do nothing; they believe
this process works; time after time
they still believe. If God forgives,
who are they to punish?

A Confusion of Wonders

After harvest in Alberta
we children of the hard God
were never certain of our sins.
We found ways to pass, but not forget,
the endless list of forbidden joys
that governed our waking.

When the CBC showed Westerns
we went next door to watch
John Wayne almost win
the very land we lived on.

But it was hard, I tell you.
Our words blurred—
Calgary . . . Calvary . . . Cavalry.

And our beds lifted at moonrise,
pushed through the window,
took off like magic flying mattresses
over cows, over wheat fields,
over horses plunging up a low hill
we wanted to name Golgotha.

THE STUD: GALAHAD, ALBERTA, 1927

(after Robert Kroetsch)

He took all his children—all, that is, except
poor Norman who would never understand this
kind of thing—and placed them in a neat row—Jim,
tallest and oldest, down to Don, the youngest—
where they had a clear view of the back corral.
The stud horse man had arrived an hour before,
had already dug a small trench in the ground,
maybe three feet deep and wide enough to back
a mare down the ramp he'd left at one end.
The stud was prancing, haltered and tethered,
rubbing against the planks of the fence, wild-eyed
and glistening. The father led the mare
blindfolded from the barn, bit tight in her mouth,
and backed her into the depression, holding
firm on the halter in case she balked or reared.
Blood flecked the froth around her muzzle.
By then the man had brought the stud and struggled
to hold it back, his horse snorting and pawing,
pissing in a noisy stream from its raw penis.
The father held the mare. The stud horse man took
his horse behind and when it reared up to mount
he gracefully ducked under the slashing hooves
and grabbed that ropey thing to guide it
into the mare. She arched her back and bared
her teeth the way the famous dying horse
did in that painting Picasso had not
yet painted. The mare screamed like a woman.
Then the stud screamed too and bit her on the neck.
The children tensed in that loud electric air
but the whole thing was over in a minute.
With this lesson done, they all went in for lunch.
The stud horse man hitched his horse to the buggy
and left for a quick stop at the bar in town.

Six Swans in a Snow Storm

I could just make them out
when the projector slipped
up and the slide didn't
drop (the show about our
family reunion
at Medicine Hat, our
trip to the mountains or
last summer's Bible camp),
when we suddenly had
to squint at the brightness,
were illuminated
by magnified white light—

six swans in a snowstorm
flying in formation
toward the far left edge
of the screen, almost snow-
blind, maybe looking for
open water, a patch
of gray against the white
that must be hidden out
there somewhere in all this
interminable light.

Hockey: An Apology

Gentle people in warmer places see
the fights and inflated salaries. They
shake their knowing heads over the blue line
blur, icing, offsides. They see ill-bred fans
beating on plexiglass, screaming for blood,
broken teeth. They won't believe the stories
about fights my grandfather witnessed
in Edmonton generations before
anyone out there could afford to go
pro. There and then fights lasted an hour, stained
the ice red. The audience stayed quiet
in the stands, grimacing as if in church.
Police carted the players off and penned
them up until they all cooled down. Farm kids,
I'd like to say, from cold places. They all became
good fathers and never beat anyone.

MEDICINE HAT: THE BEGINNING

for Lorne Taylor

Winds of the Windy City come out
of the prairie, all the way from
Medicine Hat.
                    —Carl Sandburg

This is where the wind is born.
It builds in the long valley
of the South Saskatchewan
and spreads up through the coulees
with their little feeder creeks
filled, in May, with snow runoff.
Marsh harriers and magpies
haunt the wind in its last stretch
before the prairie grasses.
It blows past howling coyotes
and sneaks around Cypress Hills,
then roars off, 2000 miles,
uninterrupted by tree
or hill until its final
good blast against Chicago.

LANDED IMMIGRANTS

No, nothing like your huddled
masses with exotic Old
World diseases. No endless
weeks aboard ship sailing to
a vague Eden. Just a rust
brown '58 Chevrolet
pulling a family of four
and a U-Haul southeast from
Moose Jaw into this foreign
land, on July Fourth. Main Street
in Portal, North Dakota,
was blocked off early; bunting
and flags were already up.
By Fargo the bands were out.
Between floats Indians rode
their nervous Appaloosas.
They looked like our Indians,
wore the same buckskins, never
looked down, and always ignored
the police, who held us up,
our motor running, until
the Minutemen with their pipes
marched past and "Yankee Doodle"
was lost in a sudden breeze.
Then the car broke down. Steam sprayed
out the grill, even seeped back
through the floorboards. The gears locked.
And Chicago, our future,
seemed an impossible dream,
a new television show
with machine guns and barrels
of illegal whiskey brought
from Canada—Chicago,
where good guys looked bad and where
gangsters finally bought it.

CELEBRATION

Even now boys go down
to muddy rivers in July.
They still strip
and wash away
Indiana sweat,
still catch bullfrogs
hiding under leaves,
stick firecrackers
into those slimy throats,
throw the bodies out
over water, and clap.

At night boys
pick house sparrows
from traps, tie tiny
bombs to bird-backs,
and let the sparrows go
free, black silhouettes
against the haze of stars.

The bombs explode in
swirls of burning feathers.

The boys celebrate Independence.

Wings fly apart.

As Close As We Will Ever Be

in memoriam: David Bray

1.
Theologies

My best friend, Dave, could never
quite believe in anything
untouchable, even though
he heard his father sing each
Sunday morning in church; old
ladies sitting in the first
pew closed their eyes and flew off
with his baritone to homes
never dreamed before. Dave thought
God stayed above and behind
us, but no matter how fast
we turned around we couldn't
catch Him; God was always
one turn ahead.

2.
If the Miracles Return

You want the miracles back again
and so do I. We memorized
them early: the sightless seeing,
the lame dancing, demons forced
from a man and disappearing
into a herd of suicidal pigs.
All that, chapter and verse, came
almost by osmosis while we

sat trapped in the last row
of that half-empty church.

Your doctors give you a month,
two, at best. That limit lives
its unspoken life in the space
between us. What can I do here?
When we boxed in the line
for the high dive twenty years ago
at Potawatomi Park, you blocked
my best punches. And laughed.
I learned to keep my distance,

and would keep it still but for this
illness that puts hand in hand
or my hand under your arm
while you walk in the pain
trying to believe the miracles
will come back. There's little
I can do here. I shave you quickly,
leaving patches of hard bristles.
I'm afraid of this touch.
It's as close as we will ever be.

First Reading

I must have already been bitten by the poetry bug or otherwise I wouldn't have walked the several miles through snow to the auditorium in the library at Notre Dame. I didn't know anyone. I was too young. I wasn't Catholic. I knew nothing, yet, about the ethics or expectations of poetry readings.

I must have already been paying enough attention to the magazines—at least to *Time, The Atlantic* and *Poetry*—to know he was something special. James Dickey. I had already shoplifted his *Poems 1957-1967* and had memorized "The Heaven of Animals."

Notre Dame was still all male then, but the intense young men were growing their beards, dressing in jeans and ripped shirts, wearing beads and peace signs. Still, I hunkered down in a corner against a wall, hoping not to be noticed, waiting for someone to call me out as a fraud—he's a kid; he's not smart enough; he's too poor; he lives in River Park, for Christ's sake; he's a Protestant! But none of the smart young men, or the professorial types in corduroy sports jackets, or the priests, or even the nuns in the first row, seemed to notice.

The lights went down and James Dickey was on stage. He was still blond in those days, but balding. Ruddy and round-faced, but not puffy like he would look later, in the photos taken after his outrageous success with *Deliverance*. Although no one else did, Dickey laughed often during the introduction, as if he couldn't believe some university type took him so seriously.

I don't remember what he read during the early part of his reading. The poems were probably those narratives about life in the South, the ones with big stuttering breaks in the middle of the lines. That was the kind of thing he was writing then. He became flushed and started sweating. In the middle of a poem he took off his sports coat and, without glancing back, handed it to the professor who had introduced him. The gesture was regal, completely confident. He loosened his tie and rolled up his sleeves while still reading the poem.

His Southern accent was thick and seemed to be getting thicker as the reading progressed. Sometimes I could barely understand him. He was cursing with regularity, and I was thrilled by it. One of the poems he read was "The Sheep Child"—and decades later I remember it more clearly than better poems read by better poets whom I have heard much more recently. Dickey introduced it by saying, "Now I'm gonna read ya'll a poem about screwin' sheep." The laughter was nervous. The nuns in the front row, who had been getting more and more agitated for half an hour, were obviously upset. Several left.

The poem started going one way, sounding a bit removed, nostalgic, almost sad—"farm boys wild to couple with anything" . . . "mounds of earth". . . "mounds of pinestraw". . . would invent stories to "keep themselves off animals." I was almost shivering with excitement. Someone could actually stand up in public, even in front of the clergy, and read a poem about bestiality and masturbation! I thought James Dickey might be arrested. But right in the middle the poem switched gears. Suddenly it became the voice of the child born after one of those couplings, when a boy couldn't keep himself away from "my mother in the long grass of the west pasture." The child—half sheep, half human—could never live. It spoke from a bottle of formaldehyde hidden on a shelf in the basement of a museum, deep "in my father's house."

When the reading was over, the audience was invited to a smaller room behind the auditorium to have a conversation with James Dickey. There were only about twenty of us, all male. There was the usual hesitant beginning, and Dickey was obviously amused by the uncertain utopian politics that colored the conversation. "Let me ask you guys some questions," Dickey said. "What ya'll gonna do in this paradise y'er gonna make?" For the most part, I don't remember what the intense young men said. One smart and brave soul went on for a while about the possibilities of finding a different way to live, a way that didn't exploit people, or animals, or environments. When this rather forced and uncomfortable conversation died out, Dickey asked, "But won't any of ya'll want to get up in the morning and just fuck?" He drawled it out.

"No, Mr. Dickey," one precise long-haired student said. "We're going to get up in the morning and make love."

"Son," the poet said, "don't knock it if ya ain't tried it."

Decades later I had occasion to exchange some e-mail with John Matthias about a poem of mine he was going to print in *The Notre Dame Review*. I mentioned the Dickey reading back in the late 60s. John told me he was the faculty member who was the advisor of record to the undergraduates who brought Dickey to Notre Dame. John wasn't overly enthusiastic about Dickey, but the students were. He remembers being shocked by the fee the poet demanded. The reading John remembers was awful. Some nuns were offended and Dickey was dead drunk. That surprised me. I didn't know anything about drunks in those days. I couldn't even recognize one. I thought he was just being a poet, but I didn't know much about them then either.

AN INTRODUCTION TO MODERN GREEK IN SOUTH BEND, INDIANA, 1967

for Vassilis Lambropoulos
Artemis Leontis
and Kostalena Michelaki

Quince and pomegranate? Sage? Rosemary?
I didn't know anyone who even knew
what those things were, so at Benner's Market
on Mishawaka Avenue, right next
to our new temple—the Gospel Center
United Missionary Church—I bought
pistachio nuts—A Product of Greece—
and Welch's White Grape Juice. I carried them
like holy food to Potawatomi
Park where at picnic tables below oaks
I read *Zorba the Greek*. I was fifteen
and there had never been a loneliness
or a longing as exquisite as mine.
I wandered over dusty hills in Crete
slaking my thirst with Welch's. I sauntered
through dark alleys in the medieval town
on Rhodes—built by the Knights Hospitaler
after Saladin conquered Jerusalem—
and smelled souvlaki grilling over fire,
eating pistachios to satisfy
my hunger. When lake effect snow began
to drift down from the sullen skies above
South Bend, I discovered Odysseus
Elytis and learned that in those poems
was some place new. But I walked there
in the sun on a beach sprinkled with white
and black pebbles, with a slightly older
dark-haired olive-skinned woman who whispered
just above the Aegean's gentle wash:
E thalassa, thalassa, thalassa.

N.B.: E thalassa = the sea. One of the most beautiful Greek words, the same word from before Homer to today's Athenian newspaper.

BORROWED LIVES

1.

Detroit Dancing, 1948

in memoriam: Leo Golus

Everyone home from the war with stories
to tell. Except me, of course. Just a bit
too young to know the horrors of Iwo,
Normandy, the Bulge, I spent the duration
peddling popcorn outside a theater on
Gratiot; later, groceries at the Market.
No woman would be wowed by any yarn
I could spin. And I'd never win a turkey
with my looks. You see, everyone needs
an angle. At the Polish National Alliance
in Hamtramck the women gathered dutifully
around their returning heroes, wide-eyed
in the presence of such courage. But when
they danced, they danced alone, their arms
circling the smoke from a hundred cigarettes.
With luck one might find another woman
anxious to show her grace. Think of it,
years spent watching two women, nineteen
or twenty, sway each other over
the stained floor. So I taught myself dancing,
downstairs, at home, in the old neighborhood,
humming "Moonlight Serenade" for rhythm,
waltzing the broom, my partner, from coal bin
to canning jars, learning to finish
with a flourish (dipping its bristled head
gently toward the cement), until I could
walk into any club anywhere in the city,
pick out any woman, turn her once

across the floor, and, if I didn't sweep
her off her feet, I'd hear at least
(and this was almost enough, then)
that I was certainly light on mine.

2.
Everything I Need

in memoriam: Teresa Golus

Poland, 1938, to Detroit, 1985

We were less
than children,
just babies.
It was before
the beginning. What
did we know?
It was Bydgoszcz
and 1938.
We all laughed
at Jews in black
coats, in black
hats, with long
strands of black
hair snaking
around their ears.
We knew nothing.

*

In another town I watched from our balcony
when they built the wall. The woman downstairs—
they took her husband first—she had two daughters,
one dark, one blonder than we were.
The blond one moved upstairs for a while,
with us, then went off to the country.
The dark one stayed below and cried.
The woman sent me out for bread and cabbage.
She told such stories—about small demons
living by bridges and stealing children,

about winged creatures smarter than God.
One morning I came down and they were gone.
My father was already dead. I don't remember him.

*

I don't know how my mother did it
in those days, but we stayed together.
Sometimes she said we were Germans
and even Janek, the baby, switched over.
Then we were Polish again and even Janek knew.
I remember stealing potatoes at night
and fighting other children to protect my brothers.
We were always together in those days.

*

I wish I remembered Dresden.
My brother does.
He tells me
about towers,
and gardens.
Churches.
I have just
one room
in one building.
It was white.
And the sound
of bombs,
and my bed shaking.
I broke my leg
playing tag
with the other
workers' children.
And there I am.
Away from Mother.
Then the bombs,

one color
for days.
No light.
No dark.
One dirty glow.
I screamed like
everyone else.
My leg hurt.
I'm eight.
Something
was happening
and my mother
doesn't come
and doesn't come.

*

My whole childhood was like that.
It would never end.
And then it ended.
We no longer had a house.
My mother stayed in the old country.
She took us, all four, to Catholic Relief.
They sent us here.
Can you believe a mother could do this?

*

I went to Iowa and lived on a farm with Mennonites.
One priest came once to give Holy Communion to the
        displaced Catholics.
I stayed two years, learned English, and ran away to my sister in Detroit.

I went to dances and even dated a Protestant doctor.
But I always knew I would marry a Polish man, a good Catholic.

And here I am.

*

I never want to leave. There is the green,
all the leaves, the shrubs, and everyone takes
care of everything. Children are safe.
Shops every mile. The old country
is nothing but hunger, the war,
running. Here almost every neighborhood
has a hospital. Grocery stores. Schools.
I have everything I need right here.

My oldest brother goes back now and then
to visit Mother. I write at Christmas,
and she sent my daughter twenty dollars
for her wedding. That's enough.
My husband and I don't travel much.
We go up north a couple times a year,
eat in good restaurants and sit by lakes.
I have everything I need right here.

A FOREIGN LANGUAGE

Whenever Rita O'Clare bowed toward her little boy to take a stone or a discarded gum wrapper from him, her shirt, damp with sweat, pulled tighter across her back. I could make out the bumpy outline of her brassiere beneath it. I could see the sweat on her neck and the damp tendrils of hair that curled up below her braid.

The little boy, Pete, almost two, was wearing only diapers under plastic baby pants. He was smearing dirt all over his legs and belly and face, and his mother didn't seem to mind. She just smiled over at him, looking hot and tired. He was playing at the edge of the parking lot beside the town's soda stand—Rose's Lemonade, Shakes, Burgers and Ice Cream—while his mother sat cross-legged on the grass beside him. I was sitting a few feet behind them on the one shaded picnic table.

It was where I had spent much of that summer, the one before my last year of high school. Usually I talked with my friends. Every so often I would pull out my comb with what I hoped was a nonchalant flourish, the way my older brother had taught me. I pulled it slowly and seriously through my hair, heavy with oil. I enjoyed combing my hair in public. It was something we all did, both the girls and the boys, although we boys had perfected a certain swaggering style of combing that we assumed made us look severe and interesting.

But this summer day was just too hot. It seemed as if anyone still left in town stayed home, probably stripped down to underwear and sitting by fans. I had no one to talk to but Rita and her little boy.

Pete climbed up on the grass, jumped on his mother's back and grabbed her braid, pulling more strands loose. Then he waddled back and forth behind her, imitating someone running. He smiled over at me as if he wanted to make sure that I noticed him. As soon as I smiled back he came over and tried climbing up on the picnic table. I reached forward and held my hand beneath him in case he slipped. He got up on the seat, stayed about ten seconds, then climbed back down. He waddled to Rita and jumped on her back again.

"He's sure lively," I called over to her.

"Yeah," she said and smiled back in her usual tired and distracted way.

"Sure livelier than me, anyway, in this heat."

"I know what you mean," she said.

"Heck, he's livelier than the whole town. Today, anyway."

"Sure," she said. "He's just a baby."

I didn't know what to say to that. I'd felt that way when I'd tried to talk with her before. I'd make a little small talk, then she would say something short, nothing impolite, just a couple of words that seemed to make sense but that didn't give me anything to respond to.

Not many people in town made the effort to talk with Rita. I don't think the town was mean, at least not any meaner than any other town. It's just that most people didn't know what to say to a woman who had a child before she was married, who never told anyone who the father was, and who decided to stay and live among us as if she was just an ordinary and usual part of the town.

If only a few of us could ever think of anything to say to her, there was, for a while anyway, a lot all of us were able to say about her. Particularly the boys in town. She was a couple of years older than me but had to drop out of school when she got pregnant. Some people thought Pete was the son of the Methodist minister's boy; the son of the Mayor's boy; the son of our grocer Bill Hendrickson, because Rita always had food; the son of Paul Simpson, the best mechanic in town, because Rita's two-tone '54 Chevy never seemed to stop running; the son of the half-breed janitor at the high school; or the son of the local baseball star who won an athletic scholarship to Michigan State where he never started a game. But as far as anyone knew Rita never told.

Her parents owned a small farm out by the Interstate, but they seldom came to town. When they did, they went to the feed store and the farm implement store and the grocery store. I never saw them visit or even talk to Rita, and in the summer she wasn't hard to find.

She spent almost every day of the warm months in front of Rose's soda stand, right out front where everyone could see her, playing with her son, seeming not to notice the usual noise and conversation that surrounded her. And after a while most of the town seemed to stop noticing her. Some of the jokes continued among the boys—"Careful, she's as horny as Rita O'Clare" or "Watch out for yourself. She's got more diseases than Rita O'Clare"—but they were never said to her. After a while even the jokes stopped.

And she stayed among us, walking through town with slightly worn clothes, pulling her little boy behind her. Unlike most of my friends I had always tried to be polite with Rita, greeting her and saying something about the weather. She never responded much, so I never tried to have long conversations. She wasn't exactly pretty, but she was well built, in proportion, although she slouched, and she had deep brown eyes that didn't seem to look at any of us. Old Mrs. Hunsperger let her live in a reconditioned garage behind her place, well-shaded and close to the corn fields that ran up against the edge of town.

Pete came back toward the picnic table where I sat and began to climb up again. I was still careful to watch him, but he got up without any trouble and sat on the edge, swinging his legs, smiling and looking at me. I leaned back, trying to look casual, smiling too. As a joke I tried to stare him down, just to look straight into those eyes, black and big, until he would look away.

He made one move as if he were changing positions and, faster than I could jump, he fell off. I think he was howling before he hit the cement. And his mother was right there, even before I sat up, not saying a word, just trying to pick him up and look at his legs. I could see the red lines of scratches running through the dirt on his knees and down into the fat skin below them.

"God, I'm sorry," I said loudly, so she could hear me above Pete's cries. "I thought he was doing fine on his own."

"It's O.K. He does this all the time."

I felt like I had committed some kind of crime, but Rita was very calm, just holding Pete's leg and already rocking him. She sat down at the table, facing me.

"I'll go get a wet rag," I said and ran through the door of the soda shop.

"Thanks," she said when I handed her the cloth.

"I'm really sorry, Rita," I said again.

"It's not your fault." She managed to smile while she held her crying child. "He's just a baby."

She held Pete with one hand and tried to clean out the scrapes with the other. Every time she touched his knee, Pete screamed again, so I offered to help. I sat down beside her and held him while she finished. I could feel the warmth from his body and the strength of his tiny bones as he writhed in my lap. His screams and his tears made me feel as if I had been responsible for his pain.

"I better take him home," Rita said while she folded the cloth, now smudged with dirt and a tinge of Pete's blood. "It's time for his nap."

"Can I help?" I asked, still feeling as if I had to do something to make up for the child's pain.

"That's O.K.," she said. "I'll manage."

"No. Really. I can carry him for you."

She looked at me and smiled again.

"O.K. If it will make you feel better."

"It will," I said, and stood up, jiggling the baby, hoping to distract him. He kept crying.

We didn't say anything the whole way to Rita O'Clare's rented garage. I felt self-conscious, half afraid that someone watching from an upstairs window might report back to my parents or my older brother that I was walking Rita and her boy home. I sweated under Pete's weight, and he clung tightly, almost desperately to my neck. He didn't even look at his mother. I was glad most of the houses we passed were dark, their blinds pulled against the heat. The only sound on the street was the insistent hiss coming from a few sprinklers.

At any other time of year we would have run into half the town on that walk, and we would have known everyone we passed. They all would have greeted us, and they all would have tried to figure out what we were doing together and why I was carrying Pete. But in early August everyone who wasn't hiding from the heat or working out at the cardboard factory on the edge of town had gone away, heading north to pine trees and lakes or at least to someplace that had swimming pools, movie theaters or tennis courts. The three of us passed through the streets on that humid day as if we were the last people left in town. It felt like someplace far away, a little bit frightening but still exciting.

When we got around behind Mrs. Hunsperger's house to Rita's place, I stopped in the shade before the open screen door, uncertain whether I should hand over the whimpering baby or carry him inside. Rita went in and held the door for me. It was almost as if I didn't have to make a decision. Once I was inside in the cooler air, she took her son from me and carried him to his crib.

Besides Pete's little bed, there was a small sink with a mirror above it, a dish rack to one side, a small refrigerator to the other, and several cupboards below. Rita's bed was in the back below a window. It was neatly made and colorful under a dark blue or deep green bedspread. There was a small card table in the middle of the room with two folding chairs and a high-chair beside it. Everything was a bit worn but very clean. I didn't notice any pictures on the wall.

"There's Coke in the fridge," she said. "Beer too, if you want one."

"Thanks." I helped myself to a bottle of Coke, tempted by the beer but not quite sure how to open the cans. I had tried pulling the tab on a beer can just once before and the beer had foamed up and over the top, soaking my pants and splashing all over the ground.

I sat at the card table watching Rita. She leaned over her baby, washing him, checking his legs, the whole time singing a song I had never heard before, one that sounded as if it might be in a foreign language. Pete still whimpered a bit, but quieted slowly while his mother sang.

When he was asleep, she walked over, just like that, for no reason I could figure out, and kissed me on the cheek. She did it as easily and as naturally as if she'd been doing it for years. It was the way my mother kissed my father when she welcomed him home in the evening.

I didn't know what to do.

Rita went to the sink and started washing her face and neck, throwing clear water over her shoulder, letting it trickle down under her shirt.

"Why do you wear so much grease in your hair?" she asked, straight out of the blue. The question made me jump. It didn't have anything to do with any of the many things that were turning around in my mind.

"I don't know." My right leg was shaking up and down in a controlled quiver. I knew I could stop it if I really wanted to, but at the moment the quivering seemed like the best thing to do. I was hoping that it looked like I was tapping my foot to some fast music only I could hear. I couldn't think of anything to say. I thought I might want to leave, but I wasn't sure.

"You'd look better without it." She walked over and touched my hair. That made me feel cold all over. I shivered. She laughed and jumped back.

"Maybe I'll try it," I said. "I've seen pictures of guys with hair like that. They always look pretty wild. You know, crazy."

She laughed again, just standing there, looking at me, with water still dripping from her face and hair. I still didn't know what to do or say, but thought maybe everything was over, that I should leave now that the baby was asleep, now that she had thanked me with that kiss on the cheek. I hadn't finished half of my coke.

When I stood up to go, she came toward me again. Her laughter had settled into a smile, soft and easy, almost loving. She looked up at me. I felt old, older than I had ever felt, and big, twice her size. I leaned down and tried to kiss her, pressing hard against her mouth, showing a strength I couldn't even name.

She pushed back, just a little, and said, "Gentle, now. Be gentle."

And we kissed again, her way, for a long time, whole minutes between breaths.

Over her shoulder I could see Pete reflected in the mirror. He was still asleep, looking like he'd never fallen, never cried, never been hurt once in his whole life. When I looked back, I saw that she had been watching me.

"I gotta go," I said.

Something flickered across her face. Later on I thought that it was just a flash of disappointment but at the time I thought she was amused, not laughing at me, just amused with me the way she might be with Pete or with a puppy.

"O.K." That was all she said. But she reached over and touched the side of my face.

"My brother's playing ball tonight. I said I'd be there."

"Sure," she said, and smiled up at me.

I don't know how I walked back to my house, but I know that I got there quickly. For hours afterward I felt a heaviness way down, some place deeper and more central than my stomach. I didn't go watch the game, and that night I fell asleep early, while I was lying on my bed trying to read *Time Magazine*. I didn't wake up until almost noon.

I avoided Rose's for the rest of the summer, staying home and reading or riding my bike far out of town on the dirt roads that disappeared between the rows of corn. I didn't want to see Rita. I didn't want Pete to let anyone know in his baby way that he knew me any better than he knew anyone else who might visit the soda stand. I didn't want his mother to tell me that I had stayed too long in her rented garage. Most of all, I didn't want her to tell me that I had left too early.

BANSHEE

I've told the story so many times
it has assumed its own truth,
how on Aranmore off Donegal
after I was fired from the hostel
and moved up to the crofter's
shack where the doctor lived,
how we stayed up almost every
night and listened to the wind
blow around us all through November.
How one night while a force nine
blew itself out against Ireland
the island girl who came to clean
every other week stayed
with us to swap stories with Doctor
Collins about heroes and the island
and fishing. We drank port waiting
for one good story to take shape.
How a scream that wasn't wind
or human, certainly not bird
or airplane, went over the shack.
I jerked fast enough to make
my glasses fly off. The doctor,
a man of science and a cynic,
was frightened too. Only the island
girl, who really did have red hair,
looked calm. "The witch of death,"
she said and—then she did it—
she chuckled. An hour later a man
came to tell us in bad English
that the woman who lived by the church
had died and would the doctor come
to sign all the necessary papers.
She was over ninety and never
left the island before her flight
this wild and ugly night.

DAYS OF 1971, 1972

Between my nights washing dishes at the restaurant
—one star in the *Michelin*—where rich folks from Toulouse
ate their quiet country dinners, and my afternoons
on the ledge below the eaves outside my little room
above the private riding club, the ledge that looked south
across green hills to the Pyrenees and where I sat
for eight months and read the expected Europeans
—Celine, of course, Baudelaire, Cavafy in the small prose
fragments of his French translation—and for the first time
understood what it was about the Americans—Poe,
Melville, Whitman, Henry Miller—how they could be sad
and exuberant on the same page and how right
that sounded to me . . . in the mornings between my job
and the reading, she would come back, often just at dawn
when the nightingales still called from the far horse pasture,
before the black mountains had whitened under their warm
Iberian sun . . . she would come back tired and smelling
of her other, more experienced lovers and would wake
me, sometimes gently caressing my beard or bringing
me back to her hard world by quietly ripping pages
from my books and dropping them on me like a blanket.

My Education in Paris

An Icelandic woman named Augusta said she wouldn't sleep with me because I was too short.

I had never asked.

A Greek woman, blonder than Augusta, said she wouldn't sleep with me because I was too thin.

I had wanted to ask her, but was too shy.

A young Persian woman, whose name meant "little white flower that grows in the desert"—at least that's what she told me and I wanted to believe her—said she wouldn't sleep with me because I was too old.

I was 22, and I hadn't asked her, either.

A French woman I did ask said she was very pleased but she preferred women.

After the Exhibition

It had been an exhibition a kid might have enjoyed; "Twelve Years of Contemporary Art in France: 1960–1972." There wasn't any particular theme or style to it. I think the artists just wanted to show that they had recovered from the American influences of the Fifties and that they were launching out in new directions.

There were many pieces where the observer became a part of the composition. Moved things. Touched them. Crawled around in them. Each piece could be as many pieces as there were people to see it. The one I enjoyed the most was a long tunnel divided into five sections. Each section was made of a screen that allowed in only one primary color. As I moved from red to blue to yellow, I felt the change in color physically, as a buzzing around the edges of my eyes and a gentle nausea in the pit of my stomach. It was like a rapid change in the weather or in the barometric pressure.

I spent most of the few francs I had left getting into the Grand Palais to see the show. I was always a bit nervous when I ran out of money but had come to expect that help would arrive when I needed it. Someone would visit me from the States and, particularly if they came to Paris before they went anywhere else in Europe, I could count on several days of food in exchange for space on the floor of my room. One of my few acquaintances in the city might give me a loan. The $100 a month my father sent me might arrive early. Occasionally I miscalculated and went hungry. A couple of months earlier I'd gone two weeks with only one glass of powdered milk and a sugar cube once a day. It had been uncomfortable, and I'd spent a lot of time in bed reading Baudelaire very slowly, but it was bearable. I wasn't afraid of being broke.

When I left the exhibition, I decided to spend the rest of my money on a beer in one of the overpriced cafés at the bottom of the Champs Elysees. I wanted to sit quietly for a while, thinking about the show and reading through the explanations of their work that several of the artists had distributed.

After a few minutes, just as I was getting comfortable and was beginning to see a pattern in all the images, an American man with a little girl sat at the table next to me. I did what I usually did in those situations: I ignored them and acted as if I couldn't understand what they were saying.

The man, dressed casually but very fashionably, was blond and looked to be in his mid-thirties. He seemed genuinely embarrassed by his lack of French. The girl was only nine or ten but still wanted coffee. They were trying to communicate to the waiter that she didn't want *café au lait* but wanted lots of milk on the side. I don't know why I did it—it was certainly not the kind of thing I usually did—but I decided to help.

"Can I translate for you?" I asked.

"Thanks," the blond man said and looked relieved. When the little girl heard me speak English, she broke into a big smile. I told the waiter to bring some espresso in a large cup with steamed milk in a pitcher. I told the girl that they made their coffee very strong here, and she should use much more milk than she ever did at home. After she had mixed the two, she said it was the best coffee she had ever tasted.

The man asked me to join them. With very little prodding, he began a quick summary of his life, even providing details of some intimacy. I'd been away from the States just long enough to have forgotten this easy kind of self-disclosure. I was even a bit embarrassed by it.

His name was Paul, the little girl's Karen. He was a lawyer in Miami. He was divorced and his wife had custody of their daughter. He got Karen for a two-week vacation every summer and spoiled her rotten, taking her wherever in the world she wanted to go. This year it was Paris. They hadn't made any plans but had just come on the spur of the moment, as quickly as their travel agent could make arrangements. Karen sat and giggled through the whole story.

I realized while Paul was talking that I had begun to miss the particularly American mixture of brashness and sentimentality. At home it got on my nerves. Its implied intimacy had made me angry occasionally, but now I found it refreshing. Much to my surprise, I liked Paul. When he offered to buy me another beer and a sandwich, I accepted.

Paul and Karen tried to pry my story from me. Although I kept some details hidden, I was comfortable enough telling them about my life in France, my studies, my friends.

"You really live here?" the little girl asked.

"Just a mile or so over there," I said, waving vaguely toward the northeast.

"Can we come visit you?"

"Oh, my place is pretty messy," I said, "and I live in a tough neighborhood."

"We don't get scared," Karen said. "We're from Miami!"

Oddly enough I felt somehow inhospitable, as if after accepting a beer from them I had to show them my room, the unmade bed, the bread crumbs, the piles of books. When Karen left to inspect the flowers planted in carefully maintained straight lines beside the street, I leaned over to Paul.

"I live in a quarter called St. Denis," I said softly to him. "It's a low-rent red light district. It might be hard to explain all those half-naked women to her."

"Yeah," he laughed. "You're right. It would."

But Paul's expression changed quickly. He looked serious and excited. He leaned toward me and whispered.

"That's not the place called Pig Alley, is it?"

I must have looked blank.

"My father was here in the war," he continued. "He told me about this place. Pig Alley. He said it had the best-looking whores in the world. Christ, he still talks about it."

It had taken me a couple of minutes to figure out the GI lingo, and when I did I laughed.

"Oh, he must mean the Place Pigalle."

"It's still here?" Paul asked. "The whores are still there?"

"Not the same ones, I hope. But, yeah, it's still here. Bigger and better than ever." I was feeling good now, like the knowledgeable tour guide to the underside of the city.

"God, I'd love to see it. I'd love to be able to tell my father about it. He would get a real kick out of it."

"I could take you," I said before I realized what I was doing. I must have been carried away with my own sense of my knowledge about the place, by the free beer, or maybe just by the conversation in English. It was not the kind of offer I usually made.

"Really? God, that would be great."

"But that's another tough part of town," I said, thinking Paul might want to head out there immediately. His daughter was running back toward us carrying a marigold she had picked. I was sure there must be some kind of fine for picking the city's flowers and looked around quickly for a gendarme. "We wouldn't want to take Karen out there."

"God, no!" he laughed. "I can get a babysitter for her at the hotel. They provide that kind of service."

Without mentioning where we were going in front of Karen, we made our plans for the evening.

"I want to go, too," she said.

"No, honey. It's going to be late. We're going to do an adult thing," Paul said, then looked at me and winked. "I'll bet the babysitter will have lots of fun things for you to do."

He gave me the name and address of his hotel. It was one of the famous expensive ones with uniformed doormen and high ornate entrances that I'd walked by but hadn't imagined I would ever find a reason to enter. I said I'd pick him up around nine. He said the evening would be on him. I left while Karen was still looking cranky but before she had a chance to start complaining.

When I knocked on Paul's hotel room door, a pretty young woman with long red hair opened it.

"Hello." I must have looked surprised.

"Don't mind me," she said. "I'm just the babysitter."

Paul was just out of the shower and wanted to dry his hair, so I talked with the young woman while Karen jumped on the bed, occasionally stopping to stare at the television.

"What are they saying?" she would ask every few minutes.

Between translations—"A bomb on a plane in Greece," or "Bad weather off the Normandy coast"—the babysitter and I swapped stories about our life in the city. Like me, like most of the young internationals I met in Paris during the early seventies, she was finding a way to scrape by. We all seemed to share a common attitude, one that mixed a sense of adventure with cynicism. Unwittingly, we looked at almost everyone we met, particularly someone as gregarious and as obviously well-off as Paul, as if they were potential marks. We seldom discussed it—we were usually too sophisticated for that—but we shared a sense of life on the fringe that turned our conversations into witty and subtle games where we all tried to gather survival information without giving anything away.

The babysitter was Irish. She did babysitting for English-speaking tourists at the more expensive hotels. It paid well, but they only used women. She was living in Paris with her boyfriend. He worked, occasionally, as a day laborer, but he didn't get work as regularly as she did.

"But he's really a poet," she said. And then added, almost defensively, although I thought I had learned not to look skeptical when people told me about their artistic ambitions, "He's a good one, too. He's beginning to publish in Ireland."

I wanted to ask more about her boyfriend's work as a day laborer. That was something I hadn't tried, and I was always looking for some way to make a few more francs. I could carry bricks and sweep floors as well as anyone. But Paul emerged from the bathroom before I had a chance. His blond hair was neatly combed. He was wearing a tailored sports coat. He looked exactly like a wealthy tourist should look. He would be an easy target for the pickpockets at the Place Pigalle.

"OK," he said. "I'm ready." We said our goodbyes quickly. Paul hugged his little girl and warned her to listen to the Irish babysitter.

Outside the hotel Paul wanted to flag a cab to take us to Pigalle, but I insisted we take the Metro.

"You'll enjoy it more," I said. "It's different."

I was right. Even though he seemed out of place among all the harried-looking Parisians on the subway, he did enjoy it. He said it made him feel a part of things. By the time we reached the Pigalle station, he was talking nonstop, but not about anything in particular. He just seemed to need an outlet for his excitement.

"I can't believe it. Less than 36 hours in Paris and I've found the place I've heard about since I was in high school. Jesus. I can't wait to tell my dad. We don't have to get any whores. . . . "

"Don't worry," I said. "I can't afford them."

" . . . but I just want to look. Walk around and look at them. God. My father was right here 25 years ago!"

When we came up in the Place, I warned Paul to move his wallet into his inside jacket pocket.

"Let's not make it too easy for them," I said.

We walked down one of the side streets, where the men wore imitation Napoleonic uniforms and called to us, where the beautiful young women stood in doorways or sat in windows, looking bored and motioning us in with half-hearted waves. At one bar, with a particularly exotic-looking Asian woman in the window, Paul wanted to go in for a drink. We sat at the bar and were immediately surrounded by four prostitutes. One stroked the inside of my thigh; another massaged my neck. Paul ordered weak champagne for all of us and paid the sixty francs happily. Of course I was aroused, but I tried to look nonchalant, as bored as the women.

One of them started whispering prices in my ear.

"You'll have to talk to my friend," I said. "He's the one with money."

As soon as the women knew that they all gathered around Paul and left me alone. Paul was flushed and laughing. He had his arms around two of the prostitutes and all of them seemed to be stroking him. He couldn't understand a word they were saying. Vivid descriptions of erotic acts, obscenities delivered with a smile, prices—everything made him laugh. I thought he would soon disappear into the back room.

Instead he drained his drink and said, "Let's go."

I shrugged to the women, who immediately looked contemptuous or hostile when they realized we were leaving, and we went out on the street.

"God!" Paul said, almost gasping. "That was wonderful. They're marvelous. That one woman had her hand in my crotch the whole time. Do you believe it? I can't wait to tell my dad."

We walked down some of the darker streets where there were women in almost every door. Paul kept talking. The women here were older and wore more makeup than the prostitutes in the bar. Paul thought they, too, were wonderful. When we passed an older woman with black hair that looked as if it were dyed, one wearing a long black evening dress, Paul stopped.

"Her," he said. "I've got to go to bed with her. Translate for me, will you? Set it up. God, I can hardly wait."

I asked the prices and the services.

"A hundred francs," I told Paul. "More if you want to do some playing around. Plus 15 for the room. She says the price is fixed. No bartering."

"Great," he said. "Let's go."

"You're on your own now. Just follow her."

"Great." He touched her arm, and she started to lead him into an unlit doorway.

"Wait," Paul called after me. "Jesus. I don't know what I was thinking." He pulled out his wallet and took out 250 francs. "Will this be enough for her?"

"It will probably make her very happy," I said.

"Here, take this." He handed me his wallet. "God, I don't want to get rolled in Paris." He laughed and walked back to the woman. "I'll meet you in the bar by the subway, OK?"

"OK."

"Great."

The small café by the Metro seemed to be the only place in the quarter without prostitutes. It was bright and dusty and almost empty. A few working men wearing soiled blue pants and jackets made from heavy, coarse cloth stood at the bar. They looked tired. I sat at a table by the front window so Paul could see me easily when he was done.

I didn't remember that I was broke until after I had ordered a beer and a Camembert sandwich. I was momentarily worried. I thought about running out into the street. Then I remembered Paul's wallet. I didn't think he would mind. I pulled it out to make sure there was enough to cover my meal.

Inside were a couple of thousand francs, including two large and ornate 500 franc notes that were folded neatly three times. Behind the French money were three 100 dollar bills.

It almost took my breath away. It was more money than I had seen at one time in years. I could live on this amount for several months, maybe half a year. At the same time as I was mesmerized by the cash, I realized that this might only be a fraction of the money Paul had brought with him for his vacation in Paris. I had forgotten people could live like this.

When the waiter came, I used one of Paul's smaller bills to pay. I left the change on the table even though the tip had been figured into the price. I felt extravagant, and extravagance felt very good.

I ate slowly. The waiter finally came by and asked if I wanted anything else. When I said that I didn't, he told me the café was going to close early. The owner's daughter was getting married the next day. He apologized.

I went outside and leaned against a lamppost. Paul should have been done by now, but I figured that the extra money he'd given the prostitute might have purchased some special services. I waited. The entrance to the Metro station was just a few yards away. People kept coming up or going down, disappearing into the ground.

I didn't think about what I did next. One minute I was just looking out over the Place Pigalle, trying to see Paul's blond hair coming toward me. He wasn't there. The next minute I had turned and was walking down into the Metro. It seemed as if a train were waiting for me. I got on and rode over to the Latin Quarter, the Place St. Michel.

St. Michel felt as if it were in another city. Another country. Another time. Young people strolled slowly through the streets. Several young men with long hair sat on the edge of the fountain in the middle of the Place. They played guitars and sang folk songs. I recognized a Dylan tune, although the singer didn't appear to know the words.

I sat at a table in the café closest to the river where I could look out and see the Metro entrance. For some reason I expected Paul to come out of it. I would walk over to him. He would laugh and tell me about his time with the prostitute, then we would drink for several hours. He would pay, of course.

Perhaps I was just being thick, but it didn't dawn on me for half an hour or so that I had taken the man's wallet and disappeared into one of the largest cities in Europe. He would never find me. I could go back to Pigalle and find him standing around looking puzzled, or I could take his wallet to his hotel. But he could never find me. I had disappeared. If he found his way back to his hotel, and he probably would, I would be nothing for him but a vaguely irritating memory.

After I finished my beer, I took the money out of Paul's wallet and stuffed it all in my pocket. I thumbed through his credit cards, his licenses and permit, his photographs. Most of them were of his daughter, smiling on a bike, smiling on a horse, smiling on a roller-coaster, smiling in New York, smiling in London, and smiling with an ocean behind her. I left everything in its place and walked out on the bridge over the Seine.

I stopped in the middle, right at the point where Notre Dame seemed the most impressive, glowing golden in its late night spotlight. I leaned against the handrail and dropped Paul's wallet down into the river. I saw its splash break the reflection from the lights illuminating the cathedral. Otherwise the river was a sparkling black. In the night it didn't look polluted or muddy. It looked as if it could have been on a postcard.

HITCHHIKING

1.
Nostalgia

I don't do it
anymore. I
hope my daughter
never does it.
It's dangerous.
I know. I've read
all about it
in the papers.

But there was once
upon a time,
between 16
and 25,
when I had no
money, a world
to see, and I'd
stick my thumb out
on any road
anywhere and
take off, sooner
or later to
parts unknown
and to places
where I would find
nothing but fun.

2.
Moose Jaw

I stood beside
the bypass past
Moose Jaw one June
day and night for
19 good hours
and 19 cars
passed me. None stopped.
I played games with
myself (OK
company out
there):

      If a car
doesn't stop in
the next hour, I'll
bury a dime.

And I did it!

If I'm still here
in two hours, I'll
tie my shoelace.

And I did it!

3.
Whitehorse

Hours from the bush,
my left foot wrapped
in bandages,

softly throbbing
from an ax wound,
I sat on my
battered suitcase
filled with dirty
socks, underwear
and too many
books, the Al-Can
Highway sending
up its dust all
over me.

      Fifteen
hundred miles to
Edmonton, then
2000 more
to Chicago.

Sure, I could do
it in a week.

I waited hours
but no long haul
truck driver stopped,
no camper, no
forestry man.
I limped back to
the bus station,
spent half my funds
for an easy
ticket heading
somewhere down south.

4.
Chateauroux

It was Sunday.
I remember
that, but I did
not see a red
castle or stream
or anything
else of interest.
The sun was out,
and I began
to feel warmer,
the Provençal
touch, even though
I wasn't half-
way to the sea.
I didn't speak
one single word
of the language,
had a couple
of friends down in
Toulouse who thought
I might show up
sometime although
they weren't certain.
I was lonely,
of course, but I
was as happy
then, for ten short
minutes, as I've
ever been, beside
a highway, south
bound, my thumb out,
broke, no one to
love anywhere

close, and nothing
to do, no one
to disappoint.

5.
Mt. Pleasant to Mishawaka

It was my last
trip, a straight shot
200 miles
south in July.
I had the chance
to see John, who
had moved west years
before, married,
calmed down, cleaned up,
started a small
company that
fixed foreign cars.
It should have been
easy, a lark.

I hadn't figured
on Grand Rapids,
a city that's
always bigger
than it should be.
I was stranded
for hours downtown,
on an exit
ramp off US
131.
I didn't cross the
Indiana
line till midnight,

saw John and his
wife for 2 hours
before they headed
back west.

        A loss . . .
but they divorced
6 months later.
And I never
again found the
gumption to hitch.

6.
What I've Become

On the first night
of snow, I drive
past a person
standing beside
the freeway, hunched
over against
the wind, one thumb
stuck out. His car
broke down; he is
wearing a suit
and tie, a long
fashionable
black coat. The fear
of hitchhiking
has moved in so
deep I don't stop.
I don't even
think about it.

For the Kids Who Yelled, "Hey, Baldy"

(after Lynch)

Remember, children, your own aging
and bring back to youth-sodden minds
this moment when your knees start
their small explosions and your backs
carry the ache of your dull futures.

Remember, O frail youth, Elisha,
tonsured and holy, who called down
two she-bears from the hills
to maul the boys who mocked his baldness.

Remember Elisha and look to the hills
because this prophet on lunch break
calls down bears, hemorrhoids,
bunions, varicose veins, corns,
impotence, and masses of gray hair
to thin the smugness of all your curls.

AND THE WATERS PREVAILED

When I was a child, I loved to water the lawn. In the evenings I would connect the hoses, turn on the outdoor faucet, and walk all around the yard, giving each inch of grass a good soaking. My parents were amused. I think they were even a little proud of me.

At some point—maybe I was nine or ten—I became interested in how the water flowed. The pressure in the hose fascinated me. I tried to guess how much water could be poured on one spot before the ground became soggy. I measured the distance between the place on the grass where I set the hose and the gutter on the street where, after a few minutes, a thin stream began flowing out of our lawn.

A few years later, when I had a bike and was able to disappear for several hours without worrying my parents, I would ride out of our subdivision, west on the unpaved roads. I passed the little creeks dredged into straight lines that drained the developments and, farther out, the man-made holding ponds that tried to contain the small springs in the countryside. After three or four miles I arrived at a place where the streams still snaked through the fields, starting in or flooding into marshes.

Then I would park my bike, climb through the fences, take my shoes off and walk out into the grasses, the mud and the water. I didn't mind the bugs. I listened for the trills of the blackbirds and their harsher calls when I got too close to their nests. The buzzing noises of the smaller birds, the wrens and the little warblers, rose from the rushes I pushed aside. Often I heard the deep clacking sounds of the birds who hid around the edge and never flew up when I walked toward them. Occasionally I watched a muskrat swimming peacefully in the deeper pools, trailing something green from its mouth. Sometimes I would stare for long minutes at my own reflection. It looked perfectly at home, unmoving and quiet.

But most of all I enjoyed the feel of water and mud around my ankles. I pulled my feet out slowly, watching the water swirl in tiny whirlpools when it flowed back into the holes I'd made. Everything else in the marsh was still. I felt that this was the way things should be.

Back home I started to think of my yard as a marsh, with mud sucking at my feet and colorful birds flying overhead. At night I began to look out my second-story window, imagining water rising from the ground, seeping into streets and yards, filling basements. The houses began to sink, the roads cracked, the ornamental shrubs and pruned maples fell over into the mire.

When I was in junior college, my parents were killed in a car accident. They had gone to a movie while I studied for my Introduction to Accounting class. They were driving home when they were rear-ended by a semi and pushed over the guardrail.

My neighbors were kind. They looked at me sadly, patted me on the back, told me how brave I was. But the house was mine. I could do whatever I needed to do. I finished my associate degree in restaurant management and got a job at the Big Boy out by the freeway. At home I began looking for the water.

I knew right away that it would take a very long time. I couldn't arouse suspicion. I brought my supplies in at night. Pumps, generators, pipes, tools. And I never bought too much from the same place. I traveled all over the city, buying some things on the east side, some up in the northern suburbs. I was careful. Patient.

It took two weeks to break through the basement floor. Then I started digging. Late at night I would put bags of dirt in the trunk of my car, open the automatic garage door, and carry the dirt far into the country. Within a month I was digging through mud. Soon after I was knee deep in water. Then I set the pipe, slowly forcing it down until I hit a pure stream. I tapped the well and began the tunnels.

I moved slowly, digging just enough space to slide through on my belly. I shored up the tunnel to protect myself from cave-ins. I often worked without light, comfortably burrowing in the dark. When I hit underground cables or the walls of my neighbors' basements, I veered around or below them. When I got a couple of hundred yards in any direction, I laid my pipes, starting the small seep holes about fifty yards away from my house. Then I slowly filled in the tunnels, packing the dirt tightly around the pipes. When I was done, I sealed my basement walls.

The tunnels and pipes took fifteen years. The work, several hours in the evening and all day on the weekends or vacations, kept me in good shape, hard and calloused. My coworkers made jokes about what they imagined was my exercise program. I always smiled.

I was polite and quiet with my neighbors. They left me alone.

When the last of the four pipes was in place, its tunnel filled and sealed, I turned the water on, just a slow trickle at first. I imagined my water seeping into the ground, rising slowly toward the yards. The neighbors didn't begin complaining about leaking basements or soggy spots in their yards until more than two years later. When they began to notice, the complaints came from up and down the block, often many houses away from the end of my pipes. Even though I had spent most of my life thinking about water, I was surprised at how far it managed to spread through the neighborhood.

By the time the city fathers decided to do something about the sogginess of our subdivision, I had finished the work inside my house. The first floor windows and doors were reinforced with steel. Late at night I practiced closing them until everything could be shut tight in less than ten minutes. In each of the six second floor windows I had carefully assembled and maintained state-of-the-art water cannons, the kind used for construction work, much more powerful than the water cannons used for crowd control. I kept them hidden behind the venetian blinds. Of course I was never able to test my cannons, but I felt confident they were ready.

On the day the city started testing the ground to find the mysterious source of the wetness, I turned on the water in the pipes full blast. Things changed quickly. In just a few days, my neighbors lawns started to cave in.

The first family left their home on the third day of full force. Their basement had filled and their driveway collapsed. Small springs were erupting from most of the lawns. Rivulets filled the gutters of the surrounding streets. The streets themselves began to crack. The story of the rising water began to appear in the newspapers.

I waited until the heavy equipment arrived. On the morning they started their serious and slightly desperate search for the source of the water, I sealed my house and turned on the cannons. First I blasted the machines, the utility lines and any police who tried to approach. I let all the families escape before I started in on their homes.

Nobody had ever seen anything like it. By the time the authorities first tried to storm my house, most of the neighborhood had been destroyed. Houses were sagging; one crumpled. All the trees were down. Water, everywhere.

On my portable radio I listened to all the reports. Even the national services were doing stories, dissecting my character, talking about the quiet loner who suddenly went berserk. Only one reporter speculated on my preparation, how many years of patient labor it must have taken to prepare my flood. After the cannons had repulsed the first police attack, I replaced even Latin American wars and European economic crises as the lead story.

The cannons have been going for ten days now. My house has begun to sag and sink. But my pipes have all held. Not a leak. The water pressure from my well is as strong as ever. Outside, past the rubble, the toppled trees and the new marsh, I see police cars and army vans.

Soon I'll have to sleep. Then they'll get me. If not the first time, then the second certainly. But I've done what I had to do. Outside, under a cloudless blue sky, the sheen of water reflects everything back to my window.

CRACK OF DAWN

Execution time. The red slash cut
between oaks, the line across snow.
One cigarette, a final cup of coffee.
It will end in rapture or holocaust
at this hour, when the world shrinks
beneath the day's weight, under the lies
about light behind an opening door,
about beginning, about birdsong.

THE COST OF A THING

Following the neon blue blaze signs—
painted on granite or nailed to birch
or pitch pine—up to the top of Burnt
Meadow Mountain in Maine and grateful
they were there to point me away from
cliffs or ridge lines leading God knows where,
I thought back to the one new trail
I made in this lifetime, maybe twelve
miles long, up from a headwater lake
of the Yukon River to a pond
at tree line. I used my ax to scalp
the bark from balsam fir and jack pine,
a clean gash on the side facing me.
On the opposite side I would cut
another gash, mirroring the first,
facing up the trail I hoped to make.
I loved the symmetry of the work.
At evening I followed my blaze
marks back to the place where I began.
A month later, walking down the trail
I'd made, I saw that every third
or fourth tree I'd blazed was dying.

GOSSAMER

in memoriam: Michael Simpson

Full summer moon and my friend
walked into the pecan orchard
below his house. Rural Georgia, 2 a.m.,
and he couldn't sleep. The heat might
have driven him out, or thirst. Perhaps
he had a premonition of early death,
or he walked at night simply because
he'd come to love that red clay country.
Jody and the boys stayed sleeping indoors.

           My friend went out
on that hill above a kudzo-bordered road
that stretched away white below the moon.

It wasn't enough for a lifetime, but that night
the moon shone through the pecan leaves
and caught the gossamers of an orchard
filled with spiders, their thin strands
of light running from branches to ground,
glistening, gently bending in the breeze,
fragile roots gone by daybreak.

THOSE INFAMOUS INLAND SHARKS

for Nicholas Wallace

They swim upriver from the big lake
long after midnight when most fish sleep,
and only at the new moon with clouds
obscuring the stars, and they have found
their secret ways around dams and weirs
until they surface in a pond below the homes
of rich folks, rising dolphinlike—
except for those child-ripping teeth,
of course, that don't even have a star
under which they could shimmer or glint—
and then they howl like no other fish
on this our dear blue earth, heard faintly
only in the sleep of restless boys.

ECOLOGICAL HISTORY IN NORTH AMERICA

for Michael Kielb

It seemed like such a simple thing—cardinals building a nest in the spruce tree out back. The male, ostentatiously red, as conspicuous as a mountain or an ocean. Easy to love. The female, perhaps more beautiful in my back yard, more appropriate: her reds muted to pinks feathered into buff brown. They brought in string and dead stalks of long grass found somewhere at the edges of lawns or in forgotten patches by fences. They didn't stop for days.

And then, suddenly, just the male chipping at neighborhood cats prowling around like panthers. He swooped in under one branch with berries or sunflower seeds in his beak and scurried out again seconds later, beak empty.

And then, nothing. No cardinals in sight. No calls. No excited chips when a cat stalked below the spruce. I finally pulled out my stepladder and climbed up to find the nest—a perfectly woven cup of grass, dark and soft on the inside. I found one egg, creamy white but heavily spotted with brown. A Jackson Pollock egg. A cowbird's egg.

Brown-headed cowbirds are nest parasites. They lay one devastating egg in the nests of smaller birds, and forget about it. The host family warms the egg and hatches the cowbird chick. Somewhere in the tricky flights and dodges of evolution, the cowbird chicks developed the behavior of hatching early, a week or so before the eggs of their adopted families. They are active and noisy, demanding food, often pushing out the eggs of their brothers and sisters, even killing the other chicks that manage to hatch.

Ornithologists speculate—but how could we ever really know such things?—that cowbirds evolved this behavior because they followed the herds of bison across the plains. One of their common names was "Buffalo Bird." Seventy million bison might have been followed by twice that many cowbirds—or three or four times that many cowbirds—picking grass seed softened in dung or insects stirred up by the undulant rivers of buffalo. The cowbirds could never stay in one place long enough to nest. Audubon couldn't figure out the behavior of cowbirds, but in a letter he wrote in

1824 he tried to find an oblique justification: "This is a mystery to me; nevertheless, my belief in the wisdom of Nature is not staggered by it."

During the last massacre of the bison, when we cut out their tongues and fried them as delicacies and left their great hulks to rot, after we tanned the last hide, even before we collected the bleached skulls and bones in railroad coal cars and sent them back east to be ground into fertilizer, there must have been a massive die-off of brown-headed cowbirds. Unnoticed in the greater mammalian stink that rose from the plains, their small bodies must have disappeared quickly into that prairie soil in the years just before it was first turned for wheat.

Cowbird survivors scattered to the small farms that had already been carved out of the woodlands. For decades few people gave them much notice as their numbers slowly increased, until they started to overwhelm the smaller songbirds. Cowbirds are particularly hard on warblers—tiny, neotropical migrants less than half as big as the birds whose chicks they must raise. Warblers try to fight back, building new nests over the ones polluted by cowbird eggs. I've seen pictures of a yellow warbler's nest, six layers deep, each layer covering the large egg waiting below it. A friend found three cowbird eggs in a warbler nest right here in town.

In northern Michigan, the only place on earth where the Kirtland's warbler nests, the Department of Natural Resources traps brown-headed cowbirds. During spring and early summer, the gray-uniformed employees of the DNR collect trapped cowbirds in plastic bags, then attach the bags to the exhaust pipes of their official-looking work trucks and gas the birds.

I was pleased when the cardinals abandoned the nest with the cowbird egg. I thought they'd build another nest somewhere in the neighborhood and get a clean start.

But a few weeks later, checking out some noisy screeching in the half-wild back lot behind my yard, I found the male cardinal—harried looking, his feathers ruffled and bedraggled—stuffing something into the maw of a cowbird chick, already much bigger than him. As soon as the chick had swallowed its food, it started squawking and dancing on its twig, pushing at the cardinal, who looked tired and worried. He set off quickly to find something else to appease this inexplicable, unappeasable child.

ALISON'S BLOND HAIR

for Alison Swan

I don't think about it often—
I'm not obsessed or anything—
but now and then, usually
in spring, I will remember
Alison's hair. It had been blond
back in those days. She cut it off,
and Dave stood at the back door, next
to my back door, and he lifted
braided strands of Alison's blond
hair into the wind, releasing
them to our frozen neighborhood.
Now, decades later, I can stand
in my yard, occasionally
imagining, usually
in spring, strands of Alison's hair
glinting from mountain ash, the elms,
or lining the nests of blue jays,
cardinals, mourning doves, robins,
or hidden deep within the oak
where squirrels haul all precious
things: children's toys, housepainting rags,
even red Tibetan prayer flags
another neighbor brought back home
from that far corner of Asia.

On the Easy Life of Saints

*(after the painting
"Saint John the Evangelist on Patmos"
by Joos van Cleve)*

All of us could choose sainthood,
get rid of ordinary
distractions—bringing the sheep
back home or washing clothes,
spreading manure on the fields
or catching fish, adding what
we can to the everyday
exchange. Sainthood does have its
compensations, after all.

Imagine getting locked up
on Patmos, for Christ's good sake,
with a couple of old books,
some blank paper, a new pen,
a distant view of the sea,
time to sit so quietly
that the birds might mistake us
for bushes—then we could all
resolve ultimate questions,
or at least catch a glimpse
of something absolutely
wonderful floating in clouds
of glory.

      Then imagine
getting a job—a good job,
not overly demanding,
a job where we could be sure
we weren't harming anyone—
a house, raising a couple

of kids to reasonable
adulthood, and imagine
the slim chance of Vision then.

We're too busy to be saints.
But if the testimony
of the ages and a few
intimations in almost
all our lives add up, then we
can hold out for our little
moments of some unearned joy
(while walking dogs, putting kids
to bed, watching snow fall, when
we get a couple of hours—
unexpectedly—to read).

Maybe that's enough. It's not
Saint John the Evangelist
on Patmos blessed with his sight
of a woman clothed in sea
colors holding a perfect
child, but it's worth something—
our ordinary vision—
and we're almost sure it's real.

First Words

I carry my serious child across the lawn
of Pinckney Square on a warm evening
of this cold summer, and a lone
herring gull circles the village.
My daughter points, makes a quiet O—
the wonder of it, one of her first words.
I can appreciate gulls too, but am
satisfied with a quick look and think
Vet's Playground with its swings, slides
and climbing bars might be more fun.
She insists, so we stop, and she watches
the full circle of the gull and its flight
away from the village until it disappears
over the hill outside town, and then,
again, she makes her word, her O.

Black Ice

Some things shouldn't frighten me. I should know better. If given half a chance at a party or over drinks, I will bore my friends with stories about ice skating across prairie sloughs forty years ago, learning how to turn quickly and handle a puck. Yet when my seven-year-old daughter and I drive down by the Huron River after a two-week cold snap and find the large pond behind Barton Dam completely frozen and carrying several families of skaters, I feel the flutter of my new and overeducated fear. Of course I let her go out on the ice. I go with her. We stare down through several inches of black ice at the plants drifting in the slight current. We hope to see a cold fish swim by. She kicks a stone across the ice, squealing with pleasure at its speed and distance. She wants to kick it all the way across, over to the marina below the rich people's homes.

That's when I get scared. I call her back and climb out on the dike above the water. She keeps kicking her stone across the ice, and I notice pressure cracks. I begin to imagine the groans and cracks of ice.

"Come on, Faith. We have to go," I call out, and she ignores me as she has done for most of her life.

I keep calling, and still she ignores me, kicking her rock across the frozen river, sliding on her feet, her knees, even her butt, laughing and laughing. I call again, more urgently, and then again. I try to sound tough and threaten loss of privileges. She kicks the rock out farther and keeps going.

METAPHOR FOR THE LONG MARRIED

Beyond familiarity
there is a small lighted space—
comfortable, bright enough
without blinding, warm enough
for relief on a cold day—
a small place surrounded
by an interesting darkness
where you travel at leisure,
a place that glows at the edge
of perception, that always
waits to take you back inside.

After Twenty Years

for Christine

We sat above the rocks
below Big Sur one spring
morning and watched snowy
egrets dance, their breeding
plumes arching backward
as they raised their yellow feet
hesitantly from the surf
before he mounted her
and egret generations
began their tentative
futures. Our kinship with
snowy egrets was nothing
grand: perhaps we understood
their single-mindedness and hoped
they felt some kind of pleasure
too. It looked as if they did.

ACKNOWLEDGMENTS

Some of this work first appeared, often in very different form, in *The Beloit Poetry Journal*, *The Bonfire Review*, *Driftwood*, *The Great Lakes Review*, *Hanging Loose*, *The Hiram Poetry Review*, *The LSA Magazine*, *Michigan Quarterly Review*, *The Notre Dame Review*, *Notus*, *Parting Gifts*, *Passages North*, *Phoebe*, *The Southern Review*, *Story*, *Witness*, and *yakima*.

"On the Easy Life of Saints" first appeared in *A Visit to the Gallery* (The University of Michigan Museum of Art, 1997).

"Black Ice" first appeared in *The Huron River: Voices from the Watershed* (The University of Michigan Press, 2001).

Some of these poems were first drafted as part of a 500-poem postcard project for The Alternative Press.

"Hockey: An Apology" was reprinted in *Sports in America* (Wayne State University Press, 1995).

"Detroit Dancing, 1948" was reprinted in *Abandon Automobile: Detroit City Poetry 2001* (Wayne State University Press, 2001).

"Those Infamous Inland Sharks" was reprinted in *Ann Arbor Writes* (Ann Arbor Public Library, 2004).

Some of these poems appeared in the chapbook *Learning to Dance* (Falling Water Books, 1985).

Some of these poems appeared in the chapbook *Weather Report* (Ridgeway Press, 1988)

Some of these poems appeared in the chapbook *Detail from the Garden of Delights* (Limited Mailing Press, 1993).

Some of these poems appeared in the chapbook *Everything I Need* (March Street Press, 1996).

Some of these poems were written while the author had grants from the National Endowment for the Arts and the Michigan Council for the Arts and Cultural Affairs, or while he had residencies with The Writer's Voice and Greenhills School. The author acknowledges the generosity of Steven Gillis.

Of all the friends, teachers, students, editors, writers and readers who have contributed to this work, none has been as sharp and as consistent a critic as Marc Sheehan. The book would likely have been better if the author had taken all of his advice.